# JUNGA
## the Dancing Yeti
### in

by Stephen Tako

illustrated by Wayne Berg

## Executive Producers

## Glen V. Freter
## Tina Passalaqua Green

## Associate Producers

Tim Prüsener & Chris Wieseler of iCatch Group, Jim Chapman, Susan M. and Jeffrey L. Carpenter, Earhart & Associates Inc., Kronenberger CPA & Company Inc., The Kemper Family, BARE Bully Awareness Resistance Education, Krysta Wallrauch, International Award Winning Voice Actor

## *Junga the Dancing Yeti in Yeti, Set, Go!* is dedicated to the following friends:

**Kaiden Graham**

**The Earhart Grandchildren**

**Jax Kronenberger**

**Lilah Marie Stouffer**

**The Carpenter Grandchildren:
Riley, Matthew, Emma, Evelyn and Oliver**

**Annabel and Nathaniel Shi**

**Rosalynn Kamaya Skillin, Raiden Roy Skillin,
Oliver Lee-Darrell Rohloff, Carson Jae Rohloff**

**Matthew and Elizabeth Wallrauch**

Junga the Dancing Yeti in Yeti, Set, Go!
Ages 4-7 Illustration Storybook

Author and Creator Stephen Tako
Illustrations & Character Designs Wayne Berg
Original conceptual designs by Peter Gullerud

Published by CONFIDENT LIFE ENTERPRISES © 2022 Stephen Tako

All rights reserved. No part of this book may be reproduced or transmitted in any form or by any means whatsoever without express written permission from the author, except in the case of brief quotations embodied in critical articles and reviews. Please refer all pertinent questions to the publisher.

Library of Congress Control Number: 2021918711

ISBN-13: 978-1-7324123-6-1

www.JungaYeti.com

"Junga?" whispered Grandma Yeti...." JUNGA! It's time to wake up."

"Ughhh, I can't go. I'm sick," replied Junga.

"Junga, you are not sick," said Grandma with a smile. "You've got football practice."

"Oh Grandma..... you're right. Just wish I wasn't so... tired," said Junga, yawning.

"Breakfast is almost ready and then off you go," said Grandma.

Junga was happy to see his friends at Central Field. He felt excited and nervous. What if he was not good at football? What if he got hurt? What if kids laughed at him?

"JUNGA!" yelled Groth and Heidi together.

"Hey Guys!" said Junga, still trying to wake up.

"Attention everyone!" said a large dark-colored bird. "My name is Coach Hawksie and I want to welcome everyone to football practice."

"OH LOOK! It's the Dancing Snow Monster! BWAHAHAHA! HARHAR-HAR!" two boars snorted and laughed at Junga.

Junga felt sad and confused. Why would two kids who didn't know him be laughing and making fun of him?

"Leave Junga ALONE!" yelled Heidi.

"Oohhh.... you gonna tell your big sister?" snorted one of the Boar twins. "BWAHAHA!"

"Ahh, pay no attention to them," said a young wolf. "I'm Weston, but everyone calls me Wes. It's nice to meet you, Junga."

"Listen up everyone!" said Coach Hawksie. "Time for warm-up exercises."

Stretching - Ready, Set, Go!...... Pushups - Ready, Set, Go!...... Jumping Jacks - Ready, Set, Go!

"It's time to pick teams," said Coach Hawksie. "Wes and Brenda are team captains."

"Brenda?!?" mumbled Heidi. "My sister better pick me."

But Heidi was the last one picked by Wes, and Brenda just laughed at her little sister before both teams learned the basic rules of football.

The team had a good time learning football that morning, but later at the playground......

"LOOK OUT! HAHAHA!" laughed Brenda and the Boars.

"HEY!" yelled Junga.

"OUCH!" cried Heidi. "Stop, that hurts!"

"Aww, you gonna tell Mommy and Daddy?" laughed Brenda. "You better not, if you know what's good for you. Coach Hawksie doesn't like crybabies either, so you better not let him see you whine and cry."

"Heidi, what's wrong with them?" asked Junga.

"Brenda and the Boar twins are just trying to upset us," answered Heidi. "Sparkles says to not let their bullying bother us."

"Hmmm… maybe Sparkles is right. Let's get some of Grandma's cookies!" squealed Junga.

"Now that's a great idea," giggled Heidi.

But the next day at football practice...

"Hey you two! We're coming after you!" sneered the Boar twins to Heidi and Junga before running over both of them.

"HAHAHA. Nothing wrong with a little fun," said Brenda.

Junga felt scared because he was being picked on by the Boars.

"I don't think I like football," said Junga to himself.

"Junga?" asked Wes. "Is everything OK?"

"Well, um…." said the nervous yeti. "Wes? Have you ever noticed that the Boar twins pick on me? I was thinking of dropping out, but my Grandma reminded me that every member of the team is important. So…. I'm here…"

"Junga! They are picking on me too!" said Heidi. "Sparkles and I didn't want to get out of bed this morning, but Brenda said only losers quit."

"Well, the team needs both of you, so thanks for coming," said Wes.

"Yeah! We're not going to let them ruin our fun," said Heidi. "Now let's play football!"

Everyone was doing their best to play well and when Groth blocked the Boar twins, Junga was able to Yeti, Set, Go down the field to score his first touchdown.

"WOOHOO!!!" yelled Junga. He was so happy as he danced a Junga Jig.

A little later when Wes had the ball again, Groth yelled "I'm open!"

"LET'S GET HIM!" yelled Brenda to the Boar twins, as they jumped onto Groth and tackled him to the ground.

"Oww. My back...." winced Groth as he laid on the field.

"TIMEOUT!" yelled Coach Hawksie. "Brenda's team would lose 15 yards on the field if we were playing an actual game today. This is called an unnecessary roughness penalty. Come on now, let's make sure to respect the rules of the game."

"All right kids," continued Coach Hawksie. "We're done for the day. I hope to see all of you at the annual Mountain Bowl football game tomorrow."

"We have a problem," said Heidi to her teammates. "It seems like Brenda's team is hurting us on purpose. They have been bothering us even when we aren't playing football."

"Heidi, you're right and I'm glad Coach Hawksie gave them a timeout," agreed Junga. "Football should be fun and getting hurt is not fun… Well, I'll see you all tomorrow at the Mountain Bowl."

Everyone was excited to see players arriving from the Mountain Football League to compete in the annual Mountain Bowl Game.

"General Condor! I didn't think I'd see you again until the spring," said a delighted Junga.

"OH!" Grandma Yeti yipped. "What a nice surprise to see you again, General!"

"King Condor and I never miss this game!" said the General, happy to see the Yeti family.

"Welcome fans and a special welcome to the All-Star MFL players!" said King Condor. "Please find your seats and let the Mountain Bowl begin!"

Junga watched the football players and what he saw surprised him. They actually helped each other stand up after being tackled.

After the game, Junga talked with General Condor and shared that some of the kids were being too rough during practice and mean on the playground too. He really hoped this would solve the problem he and Heidi were having with some of the other children.

The General talked to Coach Hawksie about sportsmanship and he let the coach know that he had heard some players were bullying others.

The next day, Brenda and Wes's teams played their first official game against each other.

"Listen up players," said Coach Hawksie. "I hope yesterday's game taught you good skills of sportsmanship. We've been hearing stories about bullying and we will not allow this to continue."

Junga was hopeful that the coach solved his problem with the other players.

During the game, each team scored points. However, the Boars tackled Junga so hard that his helmet came off. The coach gave Brenda's team a 15 yard penalty.

"Groth," said Wes. "We need you to go in between the Boar twins to separate them so Junga has a chance to get through. Molly, you cover Brenda."

"Got it, Wes!" replied a determined Molly McMoose. "Brenda will be no trouble at all."

"Everyone else, you know your positions," continued Wes.

Wes's plan worked! Molly McMoose was able to sack Brenda before she could throw the ball.

Coach Hawksie called out for all players to take a water break.

"You guys are weak! Bunch of babies. If you don't win this game, I'm gonna get you!" said an older boy who sounded really scary.

Heidi remembered seeing this boy at the field a few times. She thought he was someone's friend, but she could see that her sister Brenda seemed nervous.

"We will win, Gus," said Brenda with a shaky voice. "We're going after the dancing yeti next."

"YOU!" yelled the brave little girl. "You are the reason my sister and others are being so mean to me and Junga! You're nothing but a big bully and we don't want you here!"

In a fit of anger, Gus flew after Heidi and Junga who were very scared of the large bird.

"You kids really need to be taught a lesson!" snarled the teenaged hawk.

"ENOUGH!" yelled Coach Hawksie who arrived just in time to help Junga and Heidi. "What is going on here?"

"Coach, I heard him threatening Brenda's team and telling them they better win the game," said Heidi who was still breathing hard from running. "I think he's the reason why they're being so mean to us all the time."

"So that explains why we've been having trouble here lately," said Coach Hawksie. "That's not how we treat children. Playing sports should be challenging and competitive but we need to teach sportsmanship - what is acceptable and what is wrong."

"I'm showing these kids how to be winners!" snapped Gus in reply.

"Intentionally hurting others and bullying them is not being a winner,"

replied the coach. "True winners play by rules that are fair and honest."

"Thank you Coach," said Junga and Heidi together.

"You're welcome," replied Coach Hawksie. "I'm sorry this happened and I'm going to have a long talk with Gus and maybe even his parents if needed. He shouldn't be bothering you again. OK EVERYONE! Let's finish the game!"

All the children learned very valuable lessons that day about playing sports responsibly, but this game wasn't over.

As Wes the Wolf threw the ball...... Yeti, Set, Go! Junga scored another touchdown and this time he danced the Junga Salsa!

"OK team," said Wes. "The game is tied and we need to get a field goal to win. Heidi, now is your chance. Are you ready?"

"Ready? I've waited my whole life for this moment!" squealed the beaming young girl.

As Heidi kicked the winning field goal, the whole team cheered, "YIPPEE!!!"

"You know what, Wes?" asked Junga. "I like football."

"I think we're going to have a great season," said Wes. "But those guys..."

"You are the worst players!" yelled Brenda to her team.

"What? No, you are," mumbled her teammates.

"Hey guys," said Wes, "we're all just learning the game."

"That's right!" added Junga. "Umm.. Come join us for pizza!"

'Yeah, Coach Hawksie just said he's treating all of us," added Heidi.

At that moment, the Boar twins realized they had something important to say to Junga and his friends.

"So like, um... it's not like we are.... um, bad... I think your dancing is cool," said the male boar named Clever to Junga.

"What my brother is trying to say," replied Trixie, the female boar, "is that we are both sorry for how we've been acting to all of you and, well.... We hope you will forgive us."

"We accept your apology," said Junga. "We would much rather have you as friends instead of having any bad feelings. Nobody is perfect and we all make mistakes."

"THAT'S RIGHT!" shouted Groth. "I would have never thought I'd be friends with a skinny girl and a YETI!"

"HEY!" laughed Heidi and Junga together.

"But serious," continued Groth. "I was a terrible bully and I did some mean things."

"But now Groth is a great friend of ours!" said Junga. "Come on everyone, let's get some pizza!"

"GOOOO TEAM!!" cheered Junga and his friends.

Junga the Dancing Yeti and his friends felt really good about how well they played as a team. After the Boar twins apologized for their behavior, they learned that forgiveness is another aspect of good sportsmanship and that win or lose, they can all get along and enjoy a meal and laugh together.

## Helpful tips from Grandma Yeti:

- Being part of a team is a commitment where each member depends on the others to show up and do their best.

- If you or your friend is being bullied, simply ignoring the bully usually doesn't help. Ask an adult to offer some advice to help you solve the problem.

- If you suspect someone is causing harm to anyone, be sure to talk to a trusted adult and share your concerns.

- When someone tells you they are sorry, forgiving them is usually the best response.

- Sportsmanship is: Fair play, respect for opponents, and gracious behavior in winning or losing.

Made in the USA
Columbia, SC
14 April 2023

14861305R00020